Mr. Dressup's Castle

Story by Paul Kropp

Art by Matt Melanson

"Keep an open mind and an open heart. Don't take life too seriously — it doesn't last forever, you know. And may I remind you for the last time, keep your crayons sharp, keep your sticky tape untangled and always put the top back on your markers."

— Ernie Coombs

CBCtelevision

Book design by Laura Brady.
Printed and bound in Canada by Friesens, Altona, Manitoba.

Library and Archives Canada Cataloguing in Publication

Kropp, Paul, 1948—
    Mr. Dressup's castle / Paul Kropp ; Matt Melanson, illustrator.

ISBN 0-660-19242-X

I. Melanson, Matt, 1977— II. Canadian Broadcasting Corporation III. Title.

PS8571.R772M713 2004   jC813'.54
C2004-903882-6

CBC
PO Box 500, Station A
Toronto, Ontario M5W 1E6

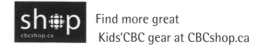

Find more great Kids'CBC gear at CBCshop.ca

Mr. Dressup and all his friends
went to the beach.

"Let's make a sandcastle and I'll make up a story," he said.

Finnegan nodded his head.

"Wow!" exclaimed Casey.
"What a great castle!"

Mr. Dressup smiled at his friends.
Then he spoke in a deep, deep voice.
"Casey, I name thee Sir Casey.
Aunt Bird, I name thee Princess
Periwinkle. You, faithful dog,
are now Sir Finnegan.
You, Alligator Al, can be
a fearsome dragon!"

"We're knights!" Casey cried.
"Isn't that great, Sir Finnegan?"

Finnegan nodded his head.

"You know what knights do, don't you?" Casey told him. "They ride big horses, rescue people who are in trouble, and get back lost treasure."

Princess Periwinkle spoke up.
"Brave knights, help me!
My treasure has been stolen
by a fearsome dragon!"

Finnegan nodded his head.

Then the magic began.

Casey and Finnegan made
a ladder from Popsicle sticks and
two long pieces of wood. Then they
put it against the side of the castle.

"Up we go," shouted Casey.
"Up, up, all the way up."

Suddenly, the ladder gave way under their weight. "Ooof!" they cried.

"I have a better idea," Princess Periwinkle told them. "Let's fold this paper to make a boat. Then we can sail across the moat and into the castle!

But when they set sail, the boat began to leak.
The water got higher and higher.
The boat sank lower and lower.
"All hands abandon ship!" Casey cried.

From the castle, they heard
the voice of Alligator Al.
"I better throw you a rope," he said.

"A very helpful dragon," Casey told Finnegan.
Soon the two knights and the princess were
climbing up the rope and into the castle.

"You'll never get this treasure!"
said the fearsome dragon.
"Oh yes, we will!" cried Sir Casey.
He pulled out a Popsicle stick
to do battle, but then the
castle began to shake!

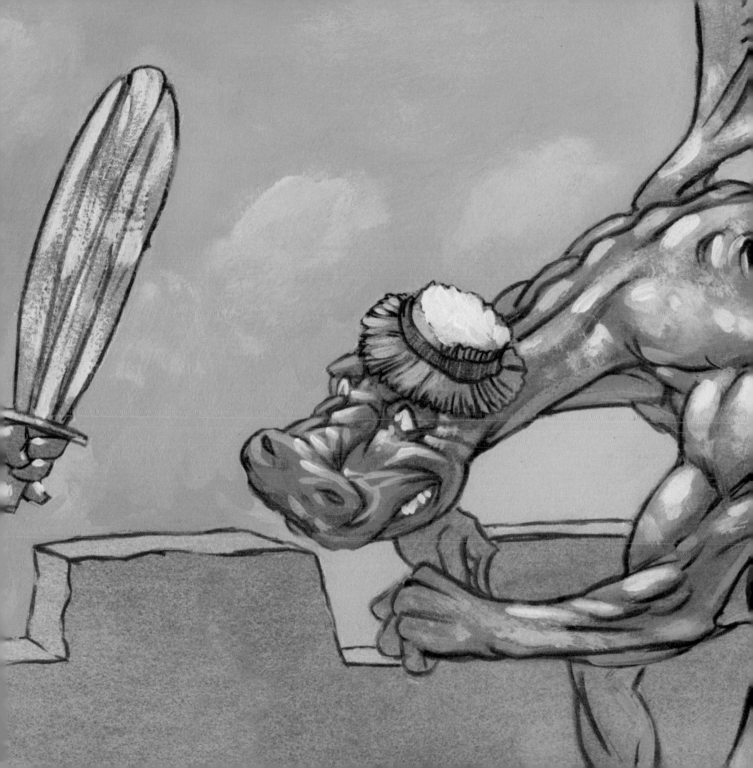

Everyone ran to the side of the castle.
"Oh, no! The tide is coming in!"
Casey told the others.
"One big wave and the whole castle will . . ."

"Sir Finnegan, Sir Casey," Mr. Dressup called down to them, "Princess Periwinkle, fearsome dragon . . . are you all right?"